Tracey West

SCHOLASTIC INC.

New York   Toronto   London   Auckland
Sydney   Mexico City   New Delhi   Hong Kong

ISBN 978-0-545-37174-2

Copyright © 2011 by Pure West Productions, Inc.

12 11 10 9 8 7 6 5 4 3 2   11 12 13 14 15 16/0

Printed in the U.S.A.   40
First Scholastic printing, September 2011

For my dad, Tom Lubben,
whose love of the James Bond books
gave me my name.

CHAPTER ONE

Wow, this place looks pretty fancy," Zack Pearce remarked as he and his parents drove up the long, tree-lined driveway.

"I still can't believe the school is giving you a full scholarship," said his mom, Natalie. "I always knew you were smart, Zack, but I never dreamed you'd go to a school as nice as this one."

In the backseat, Zack stuck his head out the open window to get a better look at the school. Five stately brick buildings formed a rough U shape on a perfect dark green lawn. The gleaming white walkways matched the white doors and shutters that stood out against the redbrick walls. The place *did* look superfancy.

"What can I say?" Zack replied with a shrug. "I guess I was born a genius."

They drove past a white wood sign that read, St. Perfidious Yearling Academy in shiny bronze letters. Small groups of students walked along the stone paths, carrying armfuls of books. They all wore the school's uniform: gray short-sleeved shirts, black shoes, and black pants or skirts.

Zack's dad, Marcus, pulled their old car up to a circular driveway by the front entrance and parked.

"We've just got to sign some paperwork," Mr. Pearce said, as he got Zack's bags from the trunk of the car. "Then I guess you're on your own."

Zack's mom grabbed him and squeezed him in a tight hug. "This is too hard. I can't believe my little babykins is out in the world all by himself. You're only twelve, Zack!"

"Twelve and a half," Zack reminded her, wiggling out of her grasp. "And please don't call me 'babykins' in public." He quickly looked around to make sure none of the other students had heard.

"You're right," his mom said, shaking her head. "But you're growing up so fast! I didn't think I'd be saying good-bye to you until you went to college. And now you're in boarding school. You'll be sleeping here, eating here, and we'll hardly get to see you."

Mrs. Pearce's words made Zack twinge with nervousness. The idea of boarding school was a little scary, and he knew he would miss his parents. But a big part of him couldn't wait to find out what it was like at the *real* St. Perfidious.

Zack followed his parents into the main hallway and waited outside while they took care of things in the office. The hall was strangely empty. Only a statue of Principal Booker was there to keep him company. Zack had met the school's principal only once before, but he thought the statue was a good likeness. He was a tall African American man with a big, bushy mustache, and in the statue, he was winking with his left eye.

Mr. and Mrs. Pearce emerged from the office and his mom squeezed Zack tightly again as they said their good-byes. Then his dad handed him an envelope.

"It's from Principal Booker," he said.

"Isn't that nice?" Mrs. Pearce remarked. "He's sent you a personal welcome message."

There was more squeezing, more good-byes, and then Zack was left alone in the hallway. He carefully opened up the envelope from Principal Booker.

QVMM UIF FBS OFYU UP UIF XJOLJOH FZF.

Zack grinned. Principal Booker had told him to expect some challenges when he first arrived, and had hinted that a knowledge of ciphers and codes would be useful. So Zack had done some studying. This looked like a simple substitution code—where one letter of the alphabet was substituted with another. He took his cell phone from his pocket and quickly typed out the alphabet on the screen to use as a reference.

He knew from the books he'd read that often, each letter in the real message would have been replaced with the one that came before it. So Zack looked at each letter in the alphabet that came *after* each letter in the note. He tried that with the first few letters: RWNN. Nope. That didn't make sense.

"How about the other way?" Zack wondered out loud, and gave it a try, checking each letter that came *before* each letter in the message. This time, it worked.

PULL THE EAR NEXT TO THE WINKING EYE.

"Got it!" Zack said, feeling pleased with himself. He had been a little worried about how he was going to make it at St. Perfidious, but solving the cipher was a good start.

Zack picked up his bags, walked to the statue, and stood on his toes to reach the left ear and give it a pull. Then he stepped back, startled, as the statue slowly began to slide to the right, revealing a metal plate underneath it marked with a red letter *X*. Zack stood on the *X*, and the platform slowly began to sink beneath the floor.

"Of course," Zack whispered. "A secret elevator."

The statue slid back over the top, and dim yellow lights on the floor lit up the tight compartment. After about thirty seconds the elevator came to a stop and the door in front of him slid open.

Zack stepped out into a gleaming white room. A dark-haired woman wearing a blue sari was there to greet him.

"Welcome to Spy Academy, Zack."

CHAPTER TWO

"**I** am Agent Lakshmi Sharma, Principal Booker's assistant," the woman informed him. "Please follow me."

Zack's heart beat quickly as Agent Sharma led him down the hall to her office. Principal Booker had said it would happen like this, but Zack hadn't quite believed him.

Zack would never forget their first meeting. Principal Booker had come to the house to offer Zack a scholarship for St. Perfidious, one of the most respected private boarding schools in the country. After talking with Zack's parents, Principal

Booker had asked to interview Zack alone.

"Zack, we check the databases of every middle school in the country, searching for potential students for our school," Booker had said in his deep voice. "You seem like an ideal candidate for St. Perfidious."

"Um, thanks," Zack had said.

Principal Booker had leaned in and stared right into Zack's green eyes.

"Zack, how would you like to become a secret agent?"

At first, Zack thought Principal Booker was joking. But he was very serious. He explained to Zack that St. Perfidious looked like a prep school to the outside world, but underneath was a top secret academy that trained kids like Zack to become superspies.

"And what if I don't want to do it?" Zack had asked.

Principal Booker held up his pen. "Then I will shine this memory device into your eyes, and you will forget this conversation entirely."

That was all Zack needed to hear. If he could

learn how to use cool gadgets like that at St. Perfidious, he just had to go.

"You won't need to use that," Zack had said. "I'm in."

That was two weeks ago, and Zack had never stopped wondering if the whole thing was a joke. But now he knew it was real—and he couldn't wait to find out what was going to happen next.

Agent Sharma's office was so neat that if a speck of dust tried to settle there, it would leave because it was so lonely. There was a slim black laptop on her white desk, and rows of file cabinets lined the walls behind her. Colorful framed prints of artwork from India—flowers, elephants, and exotic palaces—kept the room from looking cold and boring.

Agent Sharma took a slim card from the top of her desk and handed it to Zack.

"Here is your *official* ID," she told him. "Make sure you have it at all times."

Zack looked at the card. It had his photo, a bar code, and the letters and numbers AIT 2411.

"How come it doesn't have my name?" Zack asked.

"You're an agent-in-training—an AIT," Sharma explained. "When and if you graduate, your documents will contain your real name. But that's a long way off."

Zack nodded, and the agent handed him a small black briefcase. "This is your spy gear," she explained. "You'll learn how to use it in your classes, and you'll get more equipment as you progress. Take good care of it. If it gets lost or stolen, you're out of luck."

Zack went to open it, but Agent Sharma stopped him. "There'll be time for that later," she said. "Dinner is at twelve hundred hours, and you need to get settled in your room before then. Leave your bags here, and I'll make sure they get to your room."

"Even the briefcase?" Zack asked. He was really eager to see what was inside.

"Even the briefcase," said Agent Sharma, smiling for the first time. "The hallway to the boys' dorm is behind door three-B. You're in room twenty-nine. Good luck."

"Thanks," Zack replied, and then he headed back out into the hallway.

When he opened the door marked 3B he suddenly realized why Agent Sharma had wished him luck. It opened up into a white room with a small, rectangular pool between the entry door and the door on the next wall. Sticking up from the pool were ten white pillars that zigzagged over the top of the water's surface.

"Well, that's easy," Zack said out loud. "I just have to walk across the pillars."

But as he stepped through the doorway, the room went dark. Then the pillars in the pool lit up one by one in a random order. Once the last pillar was lit, the lights came back on and the glow from the pillars faded.

"Okaaaay," Zack said uncertainly. He had a sinking feeling that the order of the pillars lighting up had something to do with how to get across the pool safely. But he had been too startled to pay attention.

"Um, could you do that again, please?" he asked loudly, hoping that whoever or whatever was controlling the room could hear him. But there was no response.

Zack considered going back to Agent Sharma and asking for help, but he knew this was another test. He'd rather fail than give up.

"Here goes," he said, taking a deep breath. He stepped out onto the pillar right in front of him. Nothing happened. Zack let out some air and grinned.

Maybe I can do this, he thought. He closed his eyes, trying to remember the light show from before. There was one pillar in front of him, and another to the right.

"I think it was this one," Zack said hesitantly, stepping forward.

Beep! Beep! Beep! Beep! A piercing alarm sounded, and Zack felt the pillar begin to lower beneath him. In seconds, he was up to his waist in cold water.

There was nothing to do but swim to the other side. He climbed up out of the pool and walked to the exit door. Zack scanned his ID card into the scanner on the side of the door. It slid open, and Zack found himself facing an older boy with red hair. The boy grinned.

"Looks like we got a fish here!"

A small crowd of boys had gathered behind him, and they were all laughing—except for one. He walked up to the red-haired boy.

"Leave him alone, Connor. That's my roommate," he said in a light accent that Zack didn't recognize. Then he turned to Zack. "I'm Mike. Don't listen to these guys. Everybody gets dunked the first day."

Mike led Zack down the hall to a door with 29 in black numerals across the top. He scanned his ID card and led Zack inside.

"I'm glad you're here," Mike told him. "My last roommate had to leave when his mom got a job in Turkey. I don't really like being alone."

"I guess it gets lonely, huh?" Zack said.

Mike shook his head. "I don't mind that. It's a security thing. It's good to have someone watch your back in this place, you know?"

Zack nodded in agreement. He was starting to get that idea.

"So I guess this is my side of the room?" Zack asked, pointing to the side of the room that contained a bed, a desk, a dresser—and nothing else. The other side was filled with at least a dozen computers, monitors, and a bunch of other blinking machines and wires.

"Yes," Mike answered. "Oh yeah, your bags are here."

Zack turned to see his bags and new briefcase neatly stacked beside the door.

"Wow, they got here fast," he said.

"That's normal," Mike assured him. "Especially if Agent Sharma's involved."

He looked at Zack. "You might want to get into your uniform," he said. "We have to head to dinner in a few minutes."

"Oh, right," Zack said, stripping off his wet clothes. "So, do I have to defuse a bomb or something to get to the dining hall? 'Cause I'm not sure if I'm up to that yet."

Mike laughed. "No worries. I have all the codes

figured out for today. Just stick with me."

Zack was feeling pretty glad he'd gotten Mike for a roommate instead of someone like that Connor guy. He quickly dressed, ran his fingers through his light brown hair, which was still wet, and followed Mike through the winding hallways of the boys' dorm to the dining hall. There were three different checkpoints along the way, and Mike got them through each one easily.

As they walked, Zack told Mike a little bit about his mom and dad and his friends back in New Jersey. Mike explained that his family was from the country of Cameroon in Africa, but they'd lived in Delaware since Mike was a baby. Zack was curious to ask Mike some questions about what it was like in Cameroon, but they had reached the dining hall.

The wide doors opened to a large room filled with students of Spy Academy. Mike led him to the food line, a long stand of metal trays filled with vegetables, fish, and piles of brown rice.

"This looks really . . . healthy," Zack said, frowning a little. He was sort of hoping for hamburgers and french fries.

"You'll get used to it," Mike assured him. "Principal Booker makes sure we eat a diet that maximizes both brain and muscle potential. It's not bad—although I'd rather eat my mom's fish stew any day."

The boys piled the food onto their plates and sat down at a table with some other boys from the school.

"Hey, it's the Fish!" Connor called out, and the other kids around him laughed.

Zack was about to announce that his name was Zack, not "the Fish," when the room got suddenly quiet. Mike nudged him, and Zack looked up to see Principal Booker standing at a lectern at the front of the room.

"Good evening, Agents-in-Training," he said. "I apologize for interrupting your meal, but I have an important announcement. I received an intelligence report this afternoon that gives me cause for concern."

"It must be important," Mike whispered to Zack. "Booker hardly ever does this."

"My sources tell me that ROGUE School has infiltrated St. Perfidious," said Principal Booker. "Someone in this room is a mole!"

CHAPTER THREE

The low murmur of shocked voices filled the room. Booker silenced them with one look.

"We are on security level five," the principal said. "Stay alert. Trust no one. We will update you with further instructions soon. But know this: We will find the mole. And when we do, the consequences will be severe."

The students didn't talk again until Booker left the dining hall, and then everybody started speaking at once.

"I don't get it," Zack said. "What's ROGUE?"

"It's a school for secret agents, like this one, but it's for bad guys," Mike explained. "ROGUE stands for Receivers of a Genuinely Unsavory Education. And get this—the guy that runs it, Maximus Booker, is Principal Booker's *brother*."

Zack let this sink in. He already thought that Principal Booker was some kind of genius, so his brother was probably really smart, too. Anyone who could get a spy into this fortress had to know what they were doing.

He looked around the dining hall. "So one of us is an enemy in disguise? That's freaky."

Mike nodded. "It could be anybody."

The best thing about Booker's announcement was that everyone forgot to tease Zack about getting soaked in the pool. Zack ate his meal unnoticed, listening to the conversations around him. Everyone had an opinion about how the spy got in, or who it could be.

Zack was finishing his last bite of brown rice when Mike nudged him. "Uh-oh," he said. "Here comes Sabina Delgado. That girl scares me."

Mike was pointing to a tall girl with long, shiny

black hair. Behind her followed a short girl with curly red hair and freckles.

Sabina sat down in the empty seat next to Zack and looked him right in the eyes. "I know you're the mole," she said directly, "so you might as well confess now."

"I don't know what you're talking about," Zack protested. "I'm not a mole. I'm from New Jersey."

"It has to be you," Sabina insisted. She held out her left hand. "Emma, the file."

The freckle-faced girl immediately handed a black file folder to Sabina.

"There have been three new students admitted to the school this month," Sabina said. "I took the liberty of researching each of you. Monica Lopez is a math genius. Harry Yi is a national martial arts champion. They're good. But you're better."

She held out a sheet of paper in front of Zack's face. "You excel in math, science, martial arts—everything. You're the perfect candidate for St. Perfidious."

"So?" Zack said. "That doesn't prove anything."

"You're good—too good to be true," Sabina

said. "Your dossier is even better than mine."

Zack shook his head. He'd been at the school for only a few hours, and now he was being accused of being some kind of double agent!

"This is ridiculous," Zack said. "You have no proof of anything."

Emma spoke up. "He's right, Sabina. This is his first day here. You should give him a chance."

"Oh, really?" Sabina said, eyeing Zack. "If he's really a genius, then why is his hair wet? A genius would be able to get across the pool." She stood up. "Emma, come on!"

Sabina quickly turned and stormed away, but Emma held back. She smiled at Zack sheepishly.

"Sabina's really cool, honest," Emma said. "She loves being an AIT so much. She'll do anything to protect this school."

Mike rolled his eyes. "She's probably just jealous. Zack is really smart, and she doesn't want the competition."

Emma shrugged. "Maybe. Listen, I'll try to keep her off your back, okay?"

Zack smiled gratefully. "Thanks."

Emma hurried off to join Sabina.

"Well, Emma was nice," Zack remarked.

"I don't know why she hangs out with Sabina," Mike said with a shrug.

After dinner, the boys went back to room twenty-nine. This time, there was no pool in the hall leading to the boys' dorm. Instead, blue laser lights crisscrossed the space, and the boys had to crawl under and step over them without setting off an alarm. Zack carefully followed Mike's every move, glad that his roommate was with him.

Once they got to the room, Mike did his homework while Zack unpacked. The first thing Zack did was open his briefcase and check out the contents. There was a pair of night-vision goggles, a small microphone that fit inside his ear and let him hear conversations from far away, a pen that emitted a laser beam, and a watch that Zack discovered was actually a minicomputer.

"Whoa," Zack said, trying out the stuff. "This is like the spy kit I got when I was eight, only a thousand times better."

"It's pretty awesome," Mike agreed, looking up

from his laptop. "And you'll get more stuff as you learn more."

Zack could have spent all night testing out his new gear, but he was pretty tired from the long day. He unpacked his clothes and then placed a brown stuffed teddy bear on his pillow.

"Nice bear," Mike remarked, but his voice was friendly, not mocking.

"Thanks," Zack said. "I know it's kinda dumb, but I've had it ever since I was a baby, you know?"

"That's cool," Mike said with a yawn. He shut off his laptop and put on a pair of headphones.

"Why are you wearing headphones to bed?" Zack asked loudly.

Mike took off the headphones. "Oh, these. While I'm sleeping, I listen to a recording that's supposed to boost my intelligence. Algorithms and stuff."

"Oh, yeah," Zack said, although he wasn't really sure what an algorithm was. "Well, good night."

Zack rolled over and grabbed his teddy bear, feeling a little silly. He was pretty sure Mr. Snuffles wasn't going to boost his intelligence.

CHAPTER FOUR

The next day, Mike showed Zack some of the cool things his watch could do during breakfast. Zack just had to tap a screen to find out what classes he had and where they were.

"It says here I have Disguise next, with someone called M. Masque," Zack announced, looking at the screen.

"I don't have Disguise until fifth period," Mike said. "But you should do okay. Masque is a little weird, but it's an easy class."

Then every watch in the dining hall beeped, announcing that breakfast was over. Zack and

Mike dropped off their trays and headed out the door.

"I almost forgot," Mike continued. "Masque does this thing with new students. You need to—" He slapped his forehead. "Oh no! I forgot my project for Tech class. I need to run back to the room."

Mike tore off down the hallway.

"What about Masque?" Zack called after him, but Mike was too frantic to answer.

Zack sighed and looked at the map on his watch. He had just three minutes to get to class. Maybe he'd be lucky and Emma would be in class with him. He could ask her what Mike was trying to warn him about.

But the only familiar face in the classroom was Sabina, who stared at him with those dark eyes as he entered the room. There was no teacher in sight. Zack nodded to a girl sitting in the front row.

"Does it matter where we sit?" he asked.

"Not in this class," she responded, and Zack sat down in the first empty seat he could find. When his watch beeped again, every seat held a student but he still didn't see the teacher.

Then everyone started to whisper, and Zack looked up to see an old woman walk through the doorway. Her face was wrinkled, her gray hair was pulled back in a bun, and she walked stooped over, leaning on a cane.

"Has anyone seen my grandson Bobby?" she asked. "I'm here for a visit."

That's strange, Zack thought. *Parents and relatives aren't supposed to be allowed in this part of the Academy.* But none of the students seemed concerned. Sabina, he noticed, was smiling.

The old woman pointed her cane right at Zack. "You, young man. Have you seen Bobby?"

"Um, no, ma'am," Zack responded politely. "I'm new here."

Everyone started laughing, and someone yelled out, "The Fish has been caught again!"

Zack frowned, confused. Then the old woman threw down her cane and stood up straight. She began to talk in a deep voice—a man's voice—with a French accent.

"And voilà! The power of disguise succeeds once again!" said the "woman." He bowed in Zack's direction. "I am your professor, Monsieur Masque. Welcome to my class!"

Zack flushed with embarrassment. The visitor wasn't an old woman after all—it was his teacher, in disguise. This was what Mike had tried to tell him.

"Um, thanks," Zack said, trying to sound casual.

"Do not be ashamed," said M. Masque. "I am the greatest master of disguise in the world! And it is only your first class."

But it was hard *not* to get discouraged, especially with Sabina nodding smugly at him. After Disguise class ended, Zack went to Stealth class. Sabina was in that class, too, but Zack was happy that Mike was also there.

The Stealth classroom was a lot neater than Masque's messy room. The floor gleamed white, the metal desks were polished, and the teacher's desk in the front of the room was bare. An American flag hung on the wall next to the whiteboard, and a leafy green plant grew in a big pot by the door.

"Thanks for trying to warn me about Masque,"

Zack said when he took his seat. "What about this Agent 4? Is he going to mess with me, too?"

"No, and it's a *she*," Mike corrected him. "But—well, you'll see."

Zack's watch beeped at the start of class, and the class went quiet. Everyone started looking around.

"What's going on?" Zack whispered to Mike.

"It's Agent 4," Mike replied. "She's a stealth expert. You never know where she is, or when she's going to appear."

"Exactly," said a female voice. "That's the whole point of stealth."

The leaves on the plant started to move, and a small woman with a head of blond curls stepped out from behind it. She wore a green dress and boots the exact color of the plant.

"Good morning!" she said brightly.

Zack turned to Mike. "That's Agent 4?"

"Shhhh," Mike warned.

Agent 4 sat at her desk, opened her briefcase, and took out a silver computer. "Now, then, everyone, open your laptops. It's time for our quiz," the teacher instructed.

Zack raised his hand, and she nodded in his direction. "Agent 4? I'm new here. My name is—"

Agent 4 cut him off, smiling. "I know who you are, AIT 2411," she said. "And I suppose you would like to get out of taking the quiz. But I'd like you to take it. That way I can see how much you already know about the art of stealth."

Even though she was smiling, she said it so firmly that Zack knew it would be pointless to argue. He opened his computer and took the quiz. As it turned out, he didn't know much about stealth at all. As soon as he entered his answers, his grade flashed on the screen: D-.

"Hmmm," said a voice behind him, and Zack turned to see Sabina scribbling in a notebook. He quickly shut his laptop so no one else would see the bad grade.

He was hoping his next class, Martial Arts, would turn out better. Mike and Emma were both in it, along with Sabina. The teacher, Ippon Sensei, was a slim Japanese woman with an aura of calmness around her. Zack changed into his martial arts *gi* in the boys' locker room and then headed into the dojo. He'd been taking karate since he was five and felt pretty confident about doing well.

"Welcome, Zack," Ippon Sensei said, bowing. Her dark brown hair was pulled back into a pony-tail, and she wore a white *gi* with a black belt. "Since you are new, I would like to assess your skills. Please step on the mat."

Zack stepped onto the black mat, scanning the students. Whom would he be facing?

"Sabina," Ippon Sensei said, "please face Zack on the mat."

Sabina walked up to Zack, and they bowed. Zack spotted a gleam in her eye that told him this wasn't going to be easy.

Ippon Sensei called for the match to start, and Zack decided to surprise Sabina with a round kick, his best move. But as soon as his leg was in the air, Sabina grabbed it and flipped him over so that he landed on the mat.

"Thank you, Sabina," Ippon Sensei said. "Zack, let's find you someone less challenging."

Zack couldn't wait for class to be over. When it

was finally time to head to the lockers and change, Emma approached him.

"How's your first day going?" she asked.

"Horrible," Zack replied. "You saw what just happened. My other classes were just as bad."

"Well, it takes some time to get used to this place," Emma said kindly.

"Nice act," said a voice behind them. It was Sabina, of course.

"What do you mean?" Zack asked.

Sabina stepped closer to him. "I know what you're up to, Zack Pearce. Nobody with your record would be doing so badly on their first day. You're just pretending to be bad at everything so nobody will think you're a mole. Well, you're not fooling me!"

CHAPTER FIVE

I can't believe Sabina thinks I'm a mole," Zack told Mike during lunch. "You don't think I'm a mole, do you?"

"It doesn't add up," Mike said. "I've got info on everybody in this place, and there are at least seven kids who I think are sneaky enough to be double agents. Not you. Besides, I like you."

"Thanks," Zack said gratefully. He took a bite of salad and then suddenly put down his fork. "Hey, I just remembered that I left something in the room. I'll see you later."

"Cool," Mike said.

Zack made his way back to the boys' dorm, and this time made it all the way to the eighth pillar before he fell into the water. By the time he dried off and put on a new uniform he realized that he had forgotten why he had come back to the room in the first place. He glanced at his watch.

"Better get to Tech class," he muttered.

The Tech classroom looked like someplace Zack really wanted to be. Devices of all kinds filled the metal shelves that lined the walls. There were no desks, just long metal worktables loaded with computers and other tools. The teacher, Dr. O, was an average-sized man with messy brown hair and thick goggles. Underneath his rumpled blue lab coat he wore a loud Hawaiian shirt. He was busy tinkering with something on one of the worktables as the class walked in.

"Oh, hey, you must be Zack," he said, looking up as Zack came in. "Take a seat on one of the stools, anywhere, anywhere. Today we'll be talking about some of the latest advances in hidden microphone technology."

Zack liked the sound of that. He eagerly took

his seat, and even nodded pleasantly to Sabina when she walked in. He was determined not to let anything go wrong in this class.

As soon as he had the thought, Principal Booker walked in with Agent Sharma.

"Sorry to interrupt," he said, "but we have a possible security breach. At the end of second period, M. Masque reported that he could not find his security clearance card. It's possible that he lost it, but just in case, we need to scan all students from his first- and second-period classes. If you are one of those students, please stand up."

Zack, Sabina, and about ten other kids stood up. Agent Sharma walked to each one and waved a gray wand that emitted blue light over each of them. Then she scanned each backpack and brief-case. When she got to him, Zack thought he saw Professor Booker eyeing him. He started to sweat.

It's just your imagination, he assured himself. *Sabina's the only one who thinks you're a spy.*

"They're all clear," Agent Sharma reported, when the last student had been scanned.

Professor Booker nodded. "Good," he said.

Then he turned to Dr. O. "A word with you outside, please."

When the adults left, Sabina approached Zack.

"Very interesting," she said. "The group of suspects has just been narrowed, and you're in it."

"That makes no sense," Zack replied. "Sharma just scanned me. If I had the card, then where is it?"

"It could be anywhere," Sabina replied. "You probably hid it someplace and will go back and get it later. Very clever, Zack. But I'll be watching you."

Everyone in class had heard Sabina's accusation, and now Zack saw them all looking at him suspiciously. He heard someone whisper the word "mole" behind his back.

CHAPTER SIX

That night, Zack worked hard to finish his homework. Agent 4 had said he could retake the Stealth quiz, and Zack wanted to get a better grade this time.

It was almost ten o'clock when he finished reading the material for the quiz. With a groan, he fell back on his bed.

Mike looked up from his laptop. "Hey, would you mind if I borrowed your computer?" he asked. "I'm downloading some new software on mine, and it's taking a while. I just need to check the Tech notes."

"Sure," Zack said, and Mike hopped off his bed to retrieve it. Even though he was exhausted, Zack decided to play around with the cipher app on his watch so he could get through breakfast in the morning. He was busy checking it out when Mike called to him.

"Hey, Zack," he said. "Did you know your computer was infected?"

Zack sat up. "No. What are you talking about?"

Mike motioned him over. "Check this out," he said. He pressed a button on the keyboard, and lines of complicated code began to scroll across the screen. "Before I logged in, I ran this security scan software I always use—you can never be too safe around here. And then I found this."

"What is it?" Zack asked.

"It's spy software," Mike explained. "It transmits all the data from your computer to a remote monitor."

"You mean somebody's hacking me?" Zack asked.

Mike nodded. "It's pretty common software, but these laptops are protected against it. This must be a really sophisticated program." He sounded impressed.

"So can you get rid of it?" Zack asked.

"Not a problem," Mike said, typing into the keyboard. Then suddenly he stopped and looked at Zack suspiciously.

"I just thought of something," he said. "What if Sabina's right? Maybe you're the spy, and you put this program in yourself so you could transmit your data back to ROGUE."

"No way!" Zack protested. "First of all, I wouldn't even know how to do that. Besides, you said you believed I wasn't a mole."

"I guess," Mike said hesitantly. "But somebody is getting this data, and who else would want it besides ROGUE?"

"You've got a point," Zack agreed. "But if I were the mole, would I really hack my *own* computer? I bet the real mole did it."

Mike nodded slowly. "That's possible. The spy software only takes thirty seconds to download."

"So if we find out who did it, we'll find the mole," Zack said.

Mike jumped up, excited. "Okay. First thing to do is check for fingerprints. Sometimes even spies get careless."

Mike rummaged through the equipment on his dresser and came back with a small black box. He took out a vial of white powder and a brush. Then he gently brushed the powder on the lid of Zack's laptop.

"Got it!" he cried. "It's loaded with prints. Most of them are probably yours. But there're a few that look different."

Mike carefully placed a piece of tape over two of the prints. When he lifted up the tape, the powder left an exact impression of the prints.

"Cool," Zack said. "But how do we know whose they are?"

"Easy," Mike said, grabbing his own laptop. "I'll have to stop my software download, but it's worth it. I've been collecting prints on everybody in this place since I came here. I've got a very detailed database."

"Don't you need mine?" Zack asked.

Mike grinned. "Got 'em already. From your

toothbrush. Now let's scan these and see what comes up."

He scanned in the first print, and Zack's ID photo appeared on the screen. Underneath, the text read, "from New Jersey," and "possible mole?"

"Hey!" Zack protested. "I thought you believed me."

"I've got to take all possibilities into account," Mike said. "But mostly, I believe you. Now let's try this other one."

He scanned it in, and the boys waited while the analysis ran. Then a photo popped up on the screen.

"It's Sabina!" Zack cried. "I knew it! She must be the mole. That's why she's been accusing *me* all this time. I've got to clear my name."

"That girls' dorm is locked down tighter than Area 51 after hours," Mike said. "Nothing's going to happen tonight. We can talk to her at breakfast."

The next morning, Zack was happy to see Sabina for the first time since he'd come to the school.

Mike followed him as he walked up to Sabina and Emma's table. Zack triumphantly thrust a card with Sabina's fingerprint on it in front of her face.

"Check out this evidence," he said. "We've got you, Sabina. You're the mole!"

Sabina looked surprised. "What are you talking about?"

"We found this fingerprint on Zack's laptop," Mike interjected. He seemed to be enjoying this as much as Zack. "Somebody installed spyware on his computer. And now we know it was you."

"You don't know anything," Sabina said, her voice as cold as steel.

Zack slipped the card into his briefcase. "Let's see what Principal Booker says about that." He turned to walk away.

"Wait!" Sabina called out. She lowered her voice. "I can explain."

Zack sat next to her. "I can't wait to hear this."

"Okay, I admit I looked at the files on your laptop," she said. "But that's only because I'm trying to find the mole. I didn't download any software."

"Pretty sloppy, leaving prints," Mike said smugly.

Sabina rolled her eyes. "Whatever. I only had a few minutes. Zack left his laptop unguarded during Disguise class. He's the sloppy one."

"Hey!" Zack protested. "You're the one who's been sneaking around. I still think you're the mole."

"And I still think *you're* the mole," Sabina shot back.

Zack shook his head. "Let's get out of here, Mike."

The boys went back to their table and ate their breakfast—a green square of some jelly-like substance that was supposed to boost brain-power. It didn't taste bad—kind of like vanilla pudding—but it looked pretty gross.

"So should we take the print to Principal Booker?" Zack asked.

Mike shook his head. "I actually believe Sabina. Besides, we need more proof."

Zack felt a tap on his shoulder. He turned to see Emma behind him.

"Hey, can I talk to you?" she asked.

"Sure," Zack said. He left the table and he and Emma walked to a quiet corner of the dining hall.

"Listen, I just want you to know that I believe Sabina," Emma said. "She loves this school so much that I know she couldn't be a double agent."

"Yeah, she does seem to be really into the whole spy thing," Zack admitted. "I get it. This school is hard, but it's way better than anything I've ever done in my life. Except maybe for Camp Ma-Ke-Ro."

"Camp what?" Emma asked.

"It's this camp I went to last summer," Zack told her. "It was really cool. There was a lake and we had karate lessons on the beach and we took nature walks and stuff. I thought that place was the best—until I came here."

Emma smiled. "Then maybe you and Sabina are more alike than you think," she said. "Sabina doesn't talk about it much, but I don't think she liked her life much before she came to

St. Perfidious. That's why I know she can't be the double agent."

"I guess that makes sense," Zack agreed, but he wasn't happy.

If Sabina hadn't hacked his laptop, then who had? And why?

CHAPTER
SEVEN

The rest of the day went pretty smoothly for Zack. His teachers no longer seemed interested in singling him out as a new student. When M. Masque walked into the classroom disguised as a Russian ballet dancer, Zack wasn't fooled.

He took the quiz again in Stealth class and this time he got a C+, which still wasn't great, but it was better than a D-. And then Agent 4 showed them this invisible powder that you could sprinkle around a secure area. If someone tried to breach the area, they would get the powder on them, but they wouldn't be able to see it unless it was exposed to an ultraviolet light. That way, the powder could link the intruder to the crime.

Ippon Sensei led them in a series of training exercises during Martial Arts and in Tech class, Dr. O taught another lesson on hidden microphones. And in his last class, Strategy, Principal Booker gave an interesting lesson on ROGUE.

"In any conflict, it's important to understand your opponent's motivations, and that is why ROGUE will always fail," Principal Booker told the class. "Maximus believes that we exist only to best him, that this is some kind of competition. But we are not in this for power or glory, like Maximus. We do this because it is what we must do."

Zack remembered what Mike had said—that Maximus was Booker's brother. That was hard to understand. How did one brother end up a good guy, and one was this terrible bad guy?

Zack was feeling pretty good about things the next morning—until Sabina approached him at breakfast. She slapped a blue folder onto the table in front of him.

Zack sighed. "What now?"

"Proof," Sabina said, her dark eyes gleaming. "I know all about that summer you spent in Camp Ma-Ke-Ro. On the outside, it looks just like an ordinary summer camp. But it's really a training ground for ROGUE agents!"

Zack couldn't believe what he was hearing. "You have got to be kidding," he said. "I was there. I know what I did. I took karate lessons and went swimming and played basketball. I went on hikes and looked for deer poop. I never learned anything about being a spy."

Sabina tapped her finger on the report. "It's all here," she said smugly. "Academy agents have been watching that camp for years."

Emma walked over. "What's going on?" she asked.

"Sabina has proof that Zack's summer camp is a ROGUE training school," Mike reported.

"It is not!" Zack insisted. "And anyway, if *everyone* knows this, like you say, then why did Principal Booker invite me here? Why would he bring someone who went to a ROGUE training camp to St. Perfidious?"

Sabina didn't have an answer to that. "I—I don't know," she said, frowning. "But I'm telling you, the evidence is here."

Zack suddenly felt angry. He was sick of being accused of something he didn't do. He looked at Emma.

"So you were just being nice to me to get information for Sabina?" he asked.

Emma's face turned red. "No, Zack, I wasn't. I swear." She looked at Sabina. "What is he talking about?"

"Sabina knew that I went to Camp Ma-Ke-Ro," Zack said. "You're the only one I told about that."

He stood up. "Sabina, you're spending all your time trying to prove I'm the mole. But I know I'm not. I'd say that means that *you* have to be the mole, and I'm going to prove it."

"You? Good luck with that," Sabina said, spinning on her heel and walking away.

Zack looked after her, glaring. "Just watch me."

CHAPTER EIGHT

All right, I got it," Mike said that night after dinner. "Now, here's what you need to do."

"So why exactly are you helping me, again?" Zack asked.

"I told you, I've never liked Sabina," Mike explained. "She's too competitive. My first week here she sabotaged an alarm I made in Tech lab and made it quack like a duck. Besides, it's a challenge, and Principal Booker says that a good agent never backs away from a challenge."

Zack nodded. "That makes sense."

"Besides, you're the one taking the big risk,"

Mike pointed out. "And if you get caught, I never helped you. Right?"

"Right," Zack replied firmly. "Okay. So what's the plan again?"

Mike held up an ID card with no picture on it. "I've been working on this as extra credit for Dr. O. It should be able to get you into any room in the girls' or boys' dorm. Tomorrow is Friday. After school, Sabina and all the other first-year girls go into town and hang out at the pizza place there. You'll have an hour, maybe an hour and a half. Get in, look through Sabina's stuff, and get out without leaving any traces behind."

"I've got my gloves," Zack told him. "I won't be leaving any prints."

Mike handed him the card. "Be careful with this, Zack. I've been working on it a long time."

"I promise," Zack said. "Thanks for helping me. Once I prove Sabina is the mole, people will stop thinking it's me."

The next day, things worked out exactly as Mike had said they would. As soon as the last class was over, the first-year girls left the building, talking and giggling. Zack waited until he was sure they were blocks away. Then he made his way to the girls' dorm.

The passage to the girls' dorm was protected by lasers that day. By now Zack was getting good at weaving his way through them without setting off the alarms. Just to be sure, he held his breath and didn't let it out until he was safely at the exit door.

"Whew," Zack sighed. So far, so good.

Next, he used Mike's card to get into the first-year hallway. His heart pounded as he flashed it across the screen. There was a beep, and the door leading to the first-year dorms opened.

Zack cautiously peered down the hall. The place was quiet, with no one in sight. Perfect. He silently made his way down to room thirty-seven and then inserted the ID card into the slot. The door slid open silently.

"Piece of cake," Zack said, grinning.

He stepped into the room—and fell flat on his face! Stunned, he realized he'd fallen over a trip wire stretched across the bottom of the door.

The wire triggered a piercing alarm that echoed loudly through the hallway. He got to his feet and turned to run, but Agent Sharma was already standing by the door.

"Hello, Zack," she said. "Come with me, please."

Zack and the agent walked in silence out of the dorms to Principal Booker's office. The sound of the alarm brought many of the students out of their rooms, and they stared and whispered as Zack walked past.

Agent Sharma escorted him right into Principal Booker's office, where Booker was sitting at his desk expectantly. Zack started to sweat. Was he going to be expelled?

"He's all yours," Sharma said to Principal Booker, and Zack swore he saw a small smile on her face. She closed the door behind her, and Zack stared in front of him, waiting to get whatever Principal Booker was going to dish out.

"I'm disappointed," Booker began. "A trip wire, really? I would think that something as simple as that wouldn't catch someone with your skills."

"I'm sorry," Zack said. "I just—"

The principal held up his hand. "I expect the students of this school to know how to accomplish a simple break-in without getting caught," he said.

Zack was stunned. Booker wasn't mad at what he had done—he was disappointed because he'd failed.

"But I'm still impressed that you got inside," he went on. "So I'll let this pass. Now, I'll take that card, please."

Zack cringed. Mike was going to be so mad! But he had no choice.

"Um, sure," he said, reaching into his pocket and handing it over.

Principal Booker examined the card. "Sophisticated work. And you did this yourself?"

Zack nodded. He had promised not to give up Mike, and at least he could still do that. "Yup. I'm a fast learner."

The principal seemed satisfied with the result. "Carry on, then," he said with a wave of his hand.

Zack gratefully got up from his seat. As he left the office, he could hear Booker mutter behind him.

"A trip wire? Honestly."

As Zack walked past Agent Sharma's office, he saw her talking to Agent 4. The word "mole" floated through the air.

Curious, Zack turned the corner and flattened himself against the wall. He reached into his pocket and took out the earbud microphone that came with his spy gear. He tucked it into his ear and pressed his ear against the wall.

"So this happened last night?" Agent Sharma asked.

"At around four hundred hours," Agent 4 replied. "Someone tried to disable the security cameras in the boys' wing, but failed."

"And they used Masque's card to do it?"

"Affirmative," replied Agent 4. "The mole must be one of the boy students. That's the only explanation."

He heard Agent Sharma sigh. "I wonder what Booker will make of this."

Zack heard movement in the room, and realized the agents might be heading out. He quickly tore down the hallway and headed back to his room.

* * *

When it was time for dinner, Zack didn't really want to go, but his stomach won out. He was starting to get used to all that healthy stuff.

Zack looked up to see Emma and Sabina approaching him.

"Listen, we're even, okay?" Zack blurted out. "You broke into my laptop, and I broke into your room."

"We're not here about that," Emma said. "I need to tell you something. About how Sabina knew about Camp Ma-Ke-Ro."

Sabina looked away.

"She planted a bug on me," Emma said. "She thought if she recorded our conversations, she could learn something to incriminate you. But best friends don't bug each other, right, Sabina?"

"I'm sorry," Sabina mumbled. Then she glared at Zack. "To Emma, but not to you."

"Fine," Zack replied. "So we're even, right?"

"Whatever." Sabina shrugged.

"Well, *I'm* sorry, Zack," Emma said. Then she smiled. "I'll talk to you later, okay?"

"Sure," Zack said, and he suddenly felt better. He may have really messed up today, but at least he knew he could trust Emma again.

CHAPTER NINE

Whooee! Whooee! Whooee! Whooee! Whooee! Whooee!

The loud alarm roused Zack out of a deep sleep. He looked at the digital clock in his room and saw it was 1:17 A.M.

There was a loud knock on the door. "Zack! Open up! It's Dr. O."

By now Mike was awake, too. He stared groggily at Zack as he got up to open the door. Dr. O was wearing plaid pajama pants and a Santana T-shirt. It was the first time that Zack had ever seen him without his goggles.

"I need you to come with me, Zack," Dr. O said. "Put on some shoes or something and let's go."

"Is something wrong?" Zack asked, hastily slipping on a pair of sneakers.

"Someone tried to break into the school's computer database," Dr. O explained. "They're using Masque's security card. We're rounding up all the boys from his first- and second-period classes."

"Good luck, Zack!" Mike called out as Zack followed Dr. O into the hallway.

As they made their way to Principal Booker's office, Zack saw teachers leading other boys there—including Connor and Harry Yi, the other new male student Sabina had mentioned.

I bet it's been him all this time, Zack thought. *Or what if it's Connor? That would be pretty cool. At least I wouldn't have to worry about him again.*

The boys sleepily stumbled to a conference room, where Agent Sharma instructed them to wait. Dr. O and Agent 4 were left behind to watch the boys as they collapsed into the metal chairs in the room.

As Zack sat down, his untied sneaker slipped

off his right foot. He reached down to put it back on, and felt something strange on the bottom of his foot.

It felt almost like powder, but when Zack examined the substance on his fingers he couldn't see anything—almost like it was invisible.

Invisible powder! Zack suddenly felt wide-awake. This was the invisible powder Agent 4 had taught them about. But what was it doing on Zack's foot?

Somebody must have planted it there—got into his room somehow and pressed the powder onto his foot to blame him for breaking into the database. But who would believe him? He had to think. . . .

Zack raised his hand. "Can I go to the bathroom, please?"

Dr. O and Agent 4 looked at each other. Dr. O shrugged.

"I'll walk him there," he said, and Agent 4 seemed satisfied.

Dr. O waited outside the door while Zack went into the boys' room. He quickly took off his sneakers, soaked a paper towel in water, and scrubbed the powder off of his feet. Then he washed his hands and put his sneakers back on.

When they got back to the conference room, Agent 4 nodded at him. "Principal Booker's ready for you."

For the second time that week, Zack found himself facing Principal Booker across his desk. This time, he was even more nervous than before.

But Booker didn't ask to see his feet. He had only one question for Zack.

"Have you ever seen this man?" he asked, holding up a photograph.

The photo showed a tall man wearing a black ninja suit. His face was unmasked, and he looked a lot like Principal Booker, except his hair was lighter and his mustache was pencil-thin instead of bushy.

A weird feeling came over Zack when he saw the photo, but he couldn't explain it. He shook it off.

"It kind of looks like you," he said. "But no, I've never seen him before."

"That's my brother, Maximus," Principal Booker explained. "He will do anything he can to stop this school and what we stand for. Do you understand?"

Zack nodded. "Yeah."

Principal Booker put down the photo. "Go back to bed, Zack."

"Okay," Zack said, confused. Was that it? But he didn't want to stick around.

Zack was quiet as Dr. O walked him back to his room. He should have been relieved about the meeting with Principal Booker. But instead, he was worried. Something about that photo of Maximus was freaking him out.

And then there was that powder. Was somebody trying to frame him? Booker seemed to have ruled out the girls as suspects, so that left out Sabina. So was it Harry Yi? And how did anybody get past Mike's security at the door?

Back in the room, he slipped off his sneakers, climbed into bed, and drifted back into a restless sleep.

"Have you ever seen this man? Seen this man? Seen this man?"

Principal Booker's words repeated in Zack's mind over and over as he slept. His dreams were haunted by Maximus Booker in his black ninja suit. The leader of ROGUE School stared at Zack with his dark eyes. Then he pointed a trumpet-shaped device at Zack, and a swirling purple light flowed from it, making Zack dizzy. Numbers, letters, and strange symbols danced in front of his eyes as a sinister laugh echoed in the background.

Zack woke with a start, drenched in sweat. The lights and the laughter were gone, but there was still a voice echoing in his head—and it was coming from his teddy bear!

Stunned, Zack picked up the bear. A deep, hypnotic voice—and somehow he knew it was Maximus Booker's—was repeating the same phrase over and over again.

"When you have the disk, bring it to the Burger Land parking lot at fourteen hundred hours on the ninth."

Zack stared at the bear, confused. He looked

over at Mike, who was sound asleep with his headphones on. Zack walked to Mike's bed and shook him awake.

Mike sat up quickly, startled. "Who's there?" he asked sleepily.

Zack pointed to his ears. "Take off your headphones."

Mike complied, and Zack held up the teddy bear. "Listen to this."

"When you have the disk, bring it to the Burger Land parking lot at fourteen hundred hours on the ninth."

Mike yawned. "Are you serious? You woke me up for a talking bear?"

"But it's not *supposed* to talk!" Zack cried. "And listen to what it's saying."

Mike was silent for a moment, and then his eyes grew wide. "Why is your bear talking about a disk?"

"I don't know," Zack admitted. "I was hoping you could help me."

Mike climbed out of bed, no longer sleepy. Zack's bear had sparked his curiosity. He took a pair of scissors from his desk.

"Don't hurt Mr. Snuffles," Zack said.

"It's the only way," Mike said seriously. He sliced open the teddy bear's back and reached inside, feeling the stuffing. Then he pulled out what looked like a small recording device.

"That is not supposed to be there," Zack insisted.

Mike plugged the device into his laptop. "Let's see." He studied the data on the screen. "It looks like this bear has been programmed to deliver a pre-recorded message every night at exactly three thirty-three in the morning. The first message started on your first night here." Mike pressed a button. "Let's listen to that one."

"Good work, Zack. You've made it inside. For your first task, you must obtain a security card from one of your instructors. Target your Disguise teacher first. His name is Monsieur Masque."

"Whoa," Mike said. He looked at Zack. "So what does this mean?"

"It means that Sabina has been right all along," Zack said. "I am the ROGUE mole!"

CHAPTER TEN

Mike jumped off his chair and put his hand on his watch. "Stay back! All I have to do is press a button and every alarm in this room will go off."

"Mike, I'm not going to hurt you!" Zack cried. "I'm not really sure what's going on. I mean, these recordings prove that I must be the mole, but honestly, I don't remember hearing them. I don't even remember meeting that Maximus guy." He sat down on the edge of his bed. "How could I be a mole and not even know it?"

The suspicious look on Mike's face vanished. "That's it! You're a sleeper agent!"

Zack frowned. "What's that?"

"That's when the bad guys take someone and program them to perform an act of sabotage," Mike explained. "The sleeper agent has no idea that they're doing anything bad. Then they steal the painting, or break into the bank, or whatever, and if they get caught, it never gets traced back to the original bad guys."

Zack slowly nodded his head. "I get it. But that is really creepy. How could I do stuff and not even remember it?"

"But it makes sense," Mike said. "You had the opportunity to steal Masque's security card in class. Then you must have hid it somewhere, which is why Sharma didn't find it on you."

Zack suddenly remembered something. "I brought it here," he realized. "I came back to the room because I thought I forgot something. Then my mind sort of went blank, and I forgot what I came back for. But I must have hid the security card somewhere in this room."

Zack knew exactly where to go. He reached under his bed and pulled out his green duffel bag. Then he unzipped the front pocket—and pulled out M. Masque's security card.

"Here it is!" he cried. "It's true, then. I *am* the mole."

"Exactly!" Mike said. "And then you used the card to try to break into the database."

Zack remembered the invisible powder on the soles of his feet. It made sense. He must have been barefoot when he tried to break into the database, and that was when he stepped in the powder.

"It all makes sense," Zack said. "So what do I do now? If I tell Principal Booker, he'll kick me out of the school."

"We could destroy the evidence," Mike suggested. "If you're not getting messages from Mr. Snuffles anymore, the spying will stop."

"And then what?" Zack asked. "What if that Maximus guy comes back for me or something? I don't want anyone else to get hurt or hypnotized or whatever because of me."

Zack and Mike stared at the laptop screen for a

few minutes, thinking. Then Zack spoke.

"I could keep being a double agent," he said.

"What do you mean?" Mike asked.

"Well, Maximus still thinks I'm a sleeper agent, right?" Zack asked, and Mike nodded. "So I'll do what he wants. I'll bring him the disk."

"Are you kidding? You can't give up the St. Perfidious database!" Mike protested.

"Of course not," Zack said. "I don't even have that. But I can give him a fake one. And then maybe I can find out some information on ROGUE that will help Principal Booker."

Mike nodded slowly. "Not bad," he said. "Now you're thinking like a secret agent, Zack!"

The boys stayed up awhile longer, making plans, before finally falling asleep. The next day was Saturday, a free day for students at the school. Zack felt nervous and excited as he got ready for his meeting with Maximus.

A half hour before the meeting time, Zack and Mike stepped out of the school onto the sunny front walk. Zack suddenly felt freaked-out.

"Maybe we should go tell Principal Booker after all," he said. "I don't know if this is such a good idea."

"I think it's a great idea."

Zack turned to see Sabina and Emma walking toward them.

"Um, what idea?" Zack asked. "I don't know what you're talking about."

"Save it, Zack," Sabina said. "I put a bug in your room two days ago. We know everything—and we're going with you."

CHAPTER ELEVEN

Mike was furious. "You've been bugging us?"

"You're lucky I did," Sabina said. "If you two think you can take on ROGUE by yourselves, you're seriously deluded. You need us."

"No way," Mike said.

"Mike, she's right," Zack admitted. "I know I can use all the help I can get. And anybody who can get a bug past your security system is worth having on our team."

Mike sighed. "All right."

"Good," Sabina said, smiling. "Now let me tell you my plan as we go."

"We already have a plan," Mike protested.

"Let's just go," Zack said impatiently. "I don't want to be late."

Burger Land, the meeting point on the teddy bear tape, was about a fifteen-minute walk away in downtown Westwick. The tree-lined streets were filled with shops and lots of places to eat, and all of them were popular with the St. Perfidious students.

It turned out that Mike and Sabina pretty much had the same plan. Mike, Sabina, and Emma would go into Burger Land and get a table with a view of the parking lot. Zack would wait three minutes and then go to the parking lot to deliver the fake disk. If anything happened, the others could see it and jump in to help.

The four of them stopped about a block before Burger Land so they could split up. To his surprise, Sabina gave him a hug.

"Good luck, Zack," she said.

Then Mike gave him a hug, too. "Yeah, what she said."

Emma shrugged. "I might as well hug you, too," she said with a smile.

Then the three students headed to Burger Land. Zack looked at his watch, waiting for three minutes to pass before he followed.

Everything that had happened was starting to sink in, and he still couldn't believe it. A week ago he was playing video games and doing regular homework at a regular school. Now he was a double agent at a supersecret spy school. It seemed so unreal.

His watch beeped, and Zack took a deep breath and headed down the sidewalk. He had to give Maximus the disk, get him to talk, and then get out of there. If everything went well, he'd have some interesting intel to bring to Principal Booker, and he'd be able to stay at St. Perfidious.

He walked into the parking lot, trying not to look at the Burger Land window so he wouldn't give up his friends. He wasn't sure exactly where to go, so he stood next to the Dumpster and waited. He scanned the cars. Maybe Maximus was in one of them, and would walk out and meet him.

Whoosh! Whoosh! Whoosh! Whoosh! Four black-clad ninja jumped down from the trees above and surrounded him. They wore black hoods, and black cloth covered most of their faces, so only their eyes were showing, and they were all about Zack's height. He knew immediately that they must be ROGUE students.

"Is Maximus around?" Zack asked. "I have something for him."

The ninja nearest to him replied with a kick to the backs of his knees. Zack fell forward, and two other ninja grabbed him by the arms.

"So, I guess he's not here?" Zack asked.

The ninja picked him up and tossed him into the Dumpster! The stench of french-fry grease and rotting lettuce overwhelmed him. Zack tried to climb out, but the Dumpster lid shut over his head.

"Help! Help! Heeeeeeeeeelp!" he cried. Where were Mike and Sabina and Emma?

There was a grinding sound, and Zack looked down to see the floor of the Dumpster opening up underneath him. A strong, unseen force pulled him down and Zack realized he was now underground, trapped in some kind of hamster tube for humans.

The powerful force in the tube pulled Zack along, taking him around turns and twists, then dropping him deeper and deeper underground. His stomach lurched as he fell—and then the tube opened up, depositing him on a concrete floor.

"Ow!" Zack complained, climbing to his feet. He brushed a pickle off his sleeve. Looking around, he saw he was in a windowless room with sleek black walls.

The space was filled with gleaming black desks and shelves loaded with computer equipment.

Maximus Booker sat behind the largest desk in the room. He wore a black business suit, black shirt, and black tie. His face looked just like it had in the photo—a younger version of Principal Booker.

"Zack. You're on time. Come closer, please," he said.

Zack slowly walked up to him, gathering every bit of courage he could find inside him.

"I have the disk, Maximus," he said.

Maximus shook his head. "Just as I thought. You have discovered you are a sleeper agent."

Zack tried not to show his surprise. "What are you talking about?"

"You used my name in the Burger Land parking lot," Maximus replied. "If you were still my sleeper agent, you wouldn't know why you were standing there."

Zack cringed. He hadn't thought of that. He searched his brain for some kind of story—anything that would get him out of here.

"It all came back to me when I saw the ROGUE ninja," he said. "But, um, no hard feelings, okay? I'll just give you the disk, find my way back, and then we can forget all about this."

Maximus laughed. "Oh, you will give me the disk. But after that, I'm afraid we disagree on the sequence of events. You see, after the disk is mine I will use my mind-control device to erase your memory of this. You will wake up at home, thinking you've been expelled from St. Perfidious, an ordinary prep school. Your parents will be disappointed, but they'll get over it."

"You can't do that!" Zack said, suddenly angry. "I never asked you to mess with my mind in the first place. Just leave me alone!"

Maximus stood up from his desk, pacing as he talked. "No, you never asked me to mess with your mind. But you were the best candidate for this operation, Zack."

"What do you mean?" Zack asked. "I still don't remember ever seeing you before this."

"But you do remember Camp Ma-Ke-Ro," Maximus told him. "Every summer, we observe the campers, hoping to find possible students for ROGUE School. Usually the ones who stand out are the strong personalities—those who dunk younger kids under the water, or put spiders in the counselors' beds. But you, Zack, you stood out in a different way."

"How?" Zack asked.

"I've never met a camper with such a weak mind," Maximus told him. "You always followed the crowd, never taking the lead. I never saw you have an original idea. You were absolutely susceptible—and the perfect candidate for my mind-control device."

Zack felt insulted. "I'm not sussept—suss—

whatever," he said. "Listen, just take the disk. I'm not going to say anything to anybody about this. Why would I? It's too embarrassing."

Maximus wasn't listening. He went on, describing his plan with relish, extremely pleased with himself.

"It was so easy," Maximus said. "You were a B and C student, so I altered your school records to make you look like a genius. I made you a martial arts expert—on paper, of course. I even made you think that you'd had Mr. Snuffles your whole life. You haven't, of course. My agents planted him in your luggage."

"Really?" Zack asked. The thought made him kind of sad.

"Your mind accepted all of it—and so did my brother, Cornelius," Maximus went on. "He didn't suspect a thing when I had the family of Mike Bilong's roommate transferred to Turkey, leaving him the only choice for your roommate. I needed to find you a roommate who wouldn't wake up when Mr. Snuffles delivered my instructions in the middle of the night."

Zack felt like a fool. He tossed the disk on Maximus's desk.

"Here, take it," he said. "Then use your mind device or whatever it is. I don't think I want to remember how stupid I was to end up being your puppet."

Maximus grinned. "That's the smartest thing I've ever heard you say, Zack."

He opened a drawer in his desk and pulled out the metal trumpet-shaped device from Zack's dreams. "This won't hurt, I promise. Just keep your eyes open, please."

Zack braced himself for the swirling purple lights. It wouldn't be so bad. At least he'd be back home with his mom and dad. And he couldn't miss Mike and Emma or even Sabina if he didn't remember them, could he?

The first purple light waves traveled toward Zack's face.

"Good-bye, Zack," Maximus said.

Then a deep voice rang through the room.

"Maximus, put that down now!"

CHAPTER TWELVE

Principal Booker slid out of the chute and marched toward Zack and Maximus. Mike, Sabina, and Emma slid out behind him. Booker tossed an object that looked like a metal boomerang at Maximus. It grabbed the mind-control device from Maximus's hands and then recoiled back to Principal Booker.

"Agents, attack!" Maximus cried.

Six ninja slid down from the ceiling on ropes and began to attack Zack and his friends. Zack ducked as one of them aimed a kick at his head. He wasn't a great fighter, but after one week of facing students in Ippon Sensei's class, he had gotten really good at dodging blows.

Luckily, Mike, Sabina, and Emma were much better. Zack watched in amazement as tiny Emma grabbed one ninja by the arm and flipped him right over! Sabina was more athletic, cartwheeling across the floor and kicking ninja in the chin as she passed them by. Mike was all about power, delivering karate chops to his opponents that sent them reeling.

As Zack somersaulted to avoid a ninja punch, he saw Maximus grab the disk and run to the back wall, pressing buttons on a control panel.

"I can always make another device, Cornelius!" he called to his brother. "But now I have all your secrets!"

The wall slid to the side and Maximus raced through the opening. The six ROGUE ninja saw their leader leave and quickly followed him.

"Should we go after them?" Sabina asked.

Principal Booker shook his head. "Let them go," he said, holding up the mind-control device. "I have what I want. And Maximus will soon find out that that disk is not what he thinks."

"What did you put on that disk, anyway?" Zack asked Mike.

Mike smiled. "Five episodes of *Yo Gabba Gabba*."

A half hour later, they all sat in Principal Booker's office back at St. Perfidious.

"So fill me in," Zack said. "How come you guys didn't come out to the parking lot when those ninja surrounded me?"

Mike looked sheepish. "Well, I ordered a Burger Meal Number Five, and I was waiting for the fries, and . . ."

"I got thrown in a Dumpster because you were waiting for fast food?" Zack asked.

Mike shrugged. "I smelled those burgers and I got weak. I've been eating brown rice for months now."

"Well, it worked out, because that's when

Principal Booker showed up," Emma chimed in.

"I don't get it. Did you call him?" Zack asked.

Sabina shook her head. "No, he just showed up at Burger Land."

"I can explain, Zack," Principal Booker said. "You see, I've always known that you were a sleeper agent."

Zack was shocked. "Really?"

The principal nodded. "We've known for a while now that Camp Ma-Ke-Ro is a front for ROGUE. At first I was genuinely interested in you as a student when I discovered your excellent school records. But when I learned you had attended the camp, my suspicions grew. We quickly learned that your records had been faked."

"Ha!" Sabina shouted triumphantly. "I knew you weren't a genius."

Zack sighed. "Yeah, I'm not even close. I can't believe I let Maximus brainwash me."

"It's not your fault, Zack," Principal Booker assured him. "Maximus's mind-control device is insidious. I've been trying to get hold of it for months now. Once we figure out the technology, we can devise a method to protect ourselves from it. That's why I let you play out your role as a sleeper agent. I knew you would lead me to it."

Zack felt a little hurt. "So you were using me, too?"

Principal Booker didn't answer right away. "I'm sorry, Zack," he said finally. "But we succeeded, and now we can make sure that this doesn't happen to anyone else."

"I guess," Zack said. That did make him feel kind of good.

"And I am grateful to your friends," Principal Booker said. "Thanks to the listening device and homing device they planted on you, we were able to figure out how to get to Maximus's hideout."

Zack looked at Mike, Sabina, and Emma. "You planted stuff on me. When?"

"When I hugged you," Sabina said. "Did you really think I would hug you for no reason?"

"Yeah, I planted the homing device when I hugged you, too," Mike said. Zack looked at Emma.

"I didn't plant anything on you," she said.

"I just felt like hugging you. You looked scared."

"Well, thanks, I guess," he said. He stood up. "I guess we should call my parents, right? I should get home."

"And why would you want to do that?" Principal Booker asked.

Zack was confused. "Don't I have to leave?"

"Why would you?" Principal Booker asked. "You're a student at this school."

"But you said so yourself—my records aren't real," Zack said. "I'm not a genius. I can't do karate. And my mind is so weak I was brainwashed by your enemy."

"Records don't always show the whole story," Principal Booker told him. "I have seen you demonstrate bravery, loyalty, and resourcefulness today. Those are some of the most important qualities a secret agent can possess. As far as I'm concerned, you have proved that you can stay here."

Zack was shocked. Mike stood up and high-fived him.

"Way to go, Zack!" he cheered.

Zack turned to Principal Booker. "I won't let you down," he promised. "I'm going to work hard, really hard. I'll become the best student at this school."

"Sorry, Zack," Sabina said with a grin. "That spot is already taken!"

ABOUT THE AUTHOR

Tracey West is the author of more than 150 books for children and young adults, including the Pixie Tricks and Scream Shop series. An avid fan of cartoons, comic books, and manga, she has appeared on the *New York Times* bestseller list as author of the Pokémon chapter book adaptations. She currently lives with her family in New York State's Hudson Valley.